Run Wild

GILL LEWIS

D1157176

I was the first one to see the wolf.

Well, Connor saw it before me, but he only saw the back of its head.

Anyway, he doesn't count because he's my younger brother.

So I, Izzy Jones, was the first one to see the wolf.

I was the first one to look it in the eye.

But what was a wolf doing in an old empty power station in the middle of London?

It just shouldn't have been there.

But then again, neither should we.

Chapter 1

We wouldn't have thought of going to the old gasworks if it weren't for the Skull brothers, Luke and Scott. Luke's in Year Ten and Scott's in Year Seven, same as me.

I've known them forever.

At primary school, Luke was always in trouble, but Scott was OK back then. He always did eco-duty with me and helped refill the bird feeders. We spent break time drawing animals all over the playground with pavement chalks.

But Scott doesn't talk to me any more.

Scott doesn't talk to anyone any more.

He doesn't come in to school much, and when he does he sticks with Luke.

Everyone says they're trouble. I heard one teacher say they live with their nan because their mum can't cope with them. Luke and Scott reckon they own everything round here. They say the skateboard park belongs to them. They've spray-painted graffiti skulls on the concrete. It's not much of a skate park – just a double ramp next to the small kids' play park – but it's all we've got. We're not allowed to skate or play ball games around our estate. It's like fun is forbidden.

Luke said no one could use the skateboard park unless they could do a flat-ground ollie. That's when you make your board do a jump from the ground into the air with you still on it.

Asha said we needed somewhere to learn our tricks. But Luke said girls couldn't skate anyway.

Asha was really mad at that. She said there was no way those Skull brothers were going to tell us what to do. And that's when we went to the old gasworks. We wanted to find somewhere to practise our skateboard moves. We wanted to show Luke and Scott that girls could skate better than them.

That's why our story really begins *before* we found the wolf. It begins with us standing outside the fence around the broken-down gasworks as we looked for a way to get in.

*

It's a hot July day.

The roads are busy with rush-hour traffic. The air is full of dust and car fumes. Drivers

hoot and toot at each other, all keen to get home. No one seems to notice us standing outside the old gasworks. I can feel sweat trickle down my back as I tug at the wire fence.

Connor pulls me back and points at a sign that says *Danger – Do Not Enter*.

"We can't go in there, Izzy," Connor says. "Mum will kill us if she finds out."

"Well, she's not going to know and you're not going to tell her," I say. "She won't be back from work until six, which is why we're stuck with you."

"I'm not going in there," he says. He folds his arms and glares at me to show me he means it.

"Well, I can always take you home," I say.

Connor looks like he might cry when I say that, and I feel bad. That was a mean thing to say. I know he doesn't want to be stuck at home with Dad. Dad lost his job six months ago, and since then he has hardly gone out. He sits at home and snaps at everything Connor and I do. He used to take us to the cinema and the park, but he doesn't any more.

Asha digs into her bag. "You can have my crisps," she says to Connor, and she holds the crisp packet up where he can't get it. She's known him all his life, and sometimes I think she knows him better than I do.

Connor frowns. "Can I have all of it?" he asks.

Asha holds it high up. "Once we're in," she says.

He kicks at the bottom of the fence and tugs at some weeds that are growing up the wire. "Through here," he says. "We can fit through this gap."

Asha and I squeeze through after him. We get stung by nettles as we shove our bags and skateboards under the wire.

"Not a word about this, Connor," I say. "Not a word to anyone."

*

The gasworks has been empty for years. Granddad told us he can remember the ships coming up the Thames to London with the coal that they burned at the gasworks to make gas for the city. The huge steel frames are part of the skyline.

For now it's a wasteland. TV companies come to film gritty crime dramas there. And I

heard someone say that the land is about to be bought up and made into shops and offices, but nothing's happened yet.

We walk around the back of one of the huge metal gas tanks. Weeds, railway tracks and rusted railway trucks stretch out before us. It's like one of those end-of-the-world movies where everyone dies and the plants have taken over.

"I didn't realise it was this big," says Asha.

"It goes on and on," I say.

Asha nudges me. "Over there. There's some flat ground by the river. We'll practise there."

Asha gives Connor her crisps, and we set our boards down on the stretch of concrete. It's uneven and weeds sprout from the smallest cracks, but no one can see us and we're free to practise.

I watch Connor walk away from us down a ramp to the river, munching on his crisps. He stands at the water's edge and pushes his toe into the line of plastic and cans that marks where the river lay at high tide.

"Stay away from the water, Con," I yell.

Asha gives me a shove. "Come on," she says, "let's show the Skull brothers what we're made of."

I put my board down behind Asha and try to follow her. It's a good thing we have our helmets and elbow- and knee-pads, because we hit the ground more times than we can count. I get better at my turns, but however hard I try I just can't get the board off the ground. "I still can't do an ollie," I shout to Asha.

Asha tries again and falls flat on her back. She sits up and looks across at me. "We'll learn," she says. "We have to."

I know she's not going to give up.

I glance at my watch and realise we've been out for ages. I'll have to get Connor home soon before Mum gets back from work.

I turn to look for him at the river's edge, but I can't see him anywhere. All I can see are ripples in the river and an empty crisp packet floating on the water. A few bubbles rise from the dark water and break the surface.

"*Connor!*" I yell. "*Connor?*"

No answer.

I begin to run down to the water. My heart is thumping. "*Connor!*" I scream. "*CONNOR!*" I

was so stupid to leave him on his own. He's not a strong swimmer.

Asha is right behind me, yelling into the water too. "CONNOR!"

I begin to panic.

"CONNNNOOOR!"

"Shhhh!" Connor's head pops out from some bushes beside me. "Shhh," he says again. "You'll scare my dinosaur."

I grab his arm. "That's not even funny."

Connor yanks himself free. "There *is* a dinosaur. An archaeopteryx. It's sitting in that bush."

"Shut up about dinosaurs," I snap. "I thought you'd drowned."

Connor's been obsessed with dinosaurs for years. He has notebooks full of his drawings of them. He knows all their names and when they lived. He even told the museum they were wrong when they put a T-rex with a stegosaurus. Connor said they could never have been seen together as they existed eighty million years apart. I know what an archaeopteryx is. It has always been Connor's favourite. It's a weird dinosaur, like a bird, with feathers and claws.

Connor looks back at me. He folds his arms and blinks back tears. "There *is* one in that bush," he says.

Asha doesn't believe him. "Come on then, dino-boy. Show us," she says.

Connor leads the way as we scramble through the branches until we come face to face with a big black bird that glares back at

us. It does look a bit like a dinosaur. It has a head like a lizard and scaly skin around its beak. Bird poo covers the ground like white paint.

"It stinks!" I say.

"It's a cormorant," says Asha. "You see loads further down the river. They stand on posts to stretch their wings out to dry."

The cormorant opens its beak wide and makes a gargling hissing sound at us.

I back away. "Come on. Let's leave it alone. We have to get home before Mum does her nut."

"Cormorant," repeats Connor. He doesn't want to go home yet.

We grab our bags and boards and head back the way we've come.

"It'll be quicker if we go this way," I say, and I lead us along an overgrown rail track, past a red-brick building. We stop to look inside. It's huge, with red-brick arches that rise high into the roof. It's cooler in there too. Afternoon sunlight falls through the broken glass windows in the ceiling. Connor runs ahead of us along the old train track and pretends to be a train.

Asha pulls me around and points. "Look," she says. "That's exactly what we need."

On the far side of the building, a long brick ramp comes down from the wall next to the river. The ramp is about twice as long and twice as high as the ramps in the skate park. I can see myself flying down it, twisting and bending around the fallen bricks.

"It's perfect," I say. I check the time. "We'll come back tomorrow."

Asha grins. "We'll show the Skull brothers that we can skate."

"Hey, Connor," I shout. "Time to go."

He's still pretending to be a train. I watch him go round the rusted tracks across the floor of the building, moving his arms like pistons. "Toot toot!" he shouts. "Toot toot!" Suddenly, he stops dead. Then he turns and starts to sprint towards us.

"*Wolf!*" he screams. When he reaches me, he grabs my arm and spins around to see if something is chasing him.

"First a dinosaur, now a wolf," I say with a sigh. "You don't think we believe you, do you?"

But Connor's hand grips my arm so tightly that I feel his fingernails dig deep into my skin.

"Wolf," he says again.

"What exactly did you see?" asks Asha.

Connor's eyes are open wide. "A wolf," he says. "I only saw the back of its head. But it's a wolf. A big grey wolf."

"Probably a dog if there's anything there at all," I say.

Asha frowns. "Let's go. I don't like dogs."

"It might be hurt," I say. I look across the building. I've always wanted to find a stray dog, take it home and ask Mum to let us keep it. "I'm going to look."

Connor holds on to me. "It's a wolf, Izzy."

"Yeah right," I say. "Let's go and see."

I walk ahead of them. Asha hangs back, holding Connor's hand. I try to look brave even if I don't feel it. What if it is a dog? It might be

dangerous. I creep along slowly and listen out for any noise.

Then I see it, about ten feet away on a pile of old sacks. It's licking its front paw. It stops and lifts its head to look at me. It's huge, bigger than any dog I've ever seen. It has rough grey fur and golden eyes. And it stares back at me. This isn't anybody's pet. It has the wild inside.

All I can do is stare while it stares back.

Connor's right.

It is a wolf.

A wolf in London.

Right here.

Right now.

Chapter 2

"Get away from it, Izzy."

I can hear the panic in Connor's voice. The top of the wolf's lip curls back to show white teeth and a pink top gum. But I can't stop looking. I can't help staring into those golden eyes. The wolf turns its head away and licks its lips.

"It wants to eat us," says Connor. "It's hungry."

"Come back," says Asha. She picks up a brick from the ground and holds it up to take aim.

"Don't," I say. "It might get angry." I edge away from the wolf, but it doesn't stand up. It doesn't look like it *can* stand up. It looks thin, with long legs and a ruff of dark fur around its neck. Maybe it's a young wolf. It doesn't look fully grown. It begins to lick its paw again and chew at one of the pads.

"Where d'you think he's come from?" I say.

"Probably escaped from a zoo," says Asha. "I'll see if one's missing." She starts to tap on her phone.

I look around the building. Maybe I can find some clues to show how the wolf got here.

Asha frowns. "I can't see anything about escaped wolves. Not yet. I'll phone my dad," she goes on. "He'll know what to do. He'll call the police or whoever comes and picks up lost wolves."

I pull her phone away before she makes the call. "Wait," I say. "No one can know."

Asha tries to snatch her phone back.

"If anyone finds out we've been in here, we'll be in big trouble," I say.

"It's a wolf," says Asha. "We've got to tell someone."

"If we do, we'll never be allowed back," I say. "We won't have anywhere to skate. We'll never be better than the Skull brothers."

Asha looks at the ramp. "So what do we do?"

"We don't have to tell anyone," I say. "We could look after the wolf ourselves." I turn to Connor. "The wolf can be like our pet. It's better than a goldfish. We always wanted a dog, didn't we?"

"Are you crazy?" says Asha. "It's a wolf."

Connor blinks hard. He stares at the wolf, but he doesn't look scared any more. He's always wanted a dog as much as me. We often look through the Dogs' Home website and send Mum and Dad links to the dogs we like. He tips his head to the side. "*Could* we keep it?"

"No," says Asha. She holds out her hand for her phone.

"Asha," I say. "What if we let it stay here for a bit? Just while we learn a few skateboard tricks."

Asha turns her skateboard over in her hands and spins the wheels. I know how much she wants to get better at skateboarding and to prove we can be better than Luke and Scott. She wants it more than me. She frowns. "What would we feed it?"

"Dog food," I say. "I've got some birthday money I can use."

"We can't just keep a wolf," says Asha. "It's dangerous."

"Have you got a better idea?" I say. "If Mum finds out I've been here with Connor, she'll ground me."

Asha sighs. "All right. We'll do your idea. For now. We won't tell anyone about the wolf until we hear where it's escaped from. But I'm not going near it."

I grin and hand back her phone. "We'll come after school tomorrow." I look at the wolf. He puts his head between his paws and watches us. "He must be hungry."

Connor digs into his bag, pulls out his lunchbox and throws his sandwich crusts near the wolf. "He can have these for now."

"We can't tell anyone about our wolf," I say.

"Not even Jakub?" says Connor. "Jakub knows all about wolves."

I shake my head. "Not even Jakub." Jakub is Connor's best friend at school. "No one can know," I say. "No one."

We can't risk anyone knowing our secret.

*

I buy some tins of dog food on the way home. When we get back, Mum's in the kitchen and Dad's sitting at the table watching TV.

He looks up. "You're late," he says.

"Just coming back from Asha's," I lie.

Mum looks across at me. "Don't leave your skateboard there, Izzy. Someone will trip on it."

23

I pick it up and push it in the cupboard under the stairs. Mum's tired, I can tell. She's taken on more shifts at the supermarket since Dad lost his job. She drains a saucepan of pasta and the steam billows up. "Tell Connor supper's ready," she says.

I serve up the pasta, and we sit around the table. The only time Dad stops looking at the TV is when Connor spills red sauce down his white shirt.

Dad glares at Connor. "Watch what you're doing," he snaps. "You're too old for a bib."

"It's OK," says Mum. She dabs the red stain with a wet cloth. "It needed a wash anyway."

Dad points his knife at Connor's plate with dinosaurs printed on. "You're too old for that stuff too."

Connor doesn't say a word. No one does.
We don't dare make a noise, not even with our
knives and forks.

I hate Dad.

When Dad lost his job, he stopped being like
the dad we knew before. It seemed like we lost
our dad too.

*

All night I think about the wolf. Is he still
there? Has someone found him?

I can't concentrate at school either. I watch
the hands on the clock crawl slowly round until
the bell rings and at last we've made it to the
end of the day.

I join everyone as they push out of the
school gates. "I'll meet you at the park," I shout
to Asha. "First I have to pick up Connor."

As I hurry along the streets, I text Mum to say we're meeting friends at the park and won't be home until after six. Connor waits for me with his teacher. He jumps up and down. He can't keep still.

Mrs Roberts, his teacher, is glad to see me. "What have you been feeding him? He's been like this all day."

I grab Connor's hand and walk with him down the road. I pull Connor forwards, but he keeps twisting and trying to look behind him.

"What's up, Connor?" I say.

"Nothing," he says.

Connor stops again. I turn to see a small boy jump into a driveway.

"Who's that, Connor?"

Connor shrugs and goes bright red. "No one."

I frown and start walking back towards the driveway. "Who is it?"

Connor runs after me. "It's just Jakub," he says. "I said he could come and see the wolf."

Jakub slides out from where he's hidden.

I glare at Connor. "You said you wouldn't tell."

"Jakub knows all about wolves," Connor insists. "He can help us."

Jakub nods his head up and down so hard I think it might come off. "My grandfather sees wolves near his farm in Poland."

"Go home, Jakub," I say.

Jakub's face falls. He pulls a big book from his bag. "I've got my book on wolves."

"Go home."

He stops and looks like he is thinking hard. "If you don't let me come," he says at last, "I'll tell."

I frown. I don't want Jakub to come with us. It's dangerous, and the less people know about our wolf the better. "What about your mum?" I ask. "Does she know where you are?"

"I said I was going with Connor to the park," he says.

"But that's not true, is it?" I say.

He looks up at me. "Does your mum know where you and Connor are going?" he asks me.

I scowl at him. I've been outsmarted by an eight-year-old. "OK," I say, "you can come too. But you've got to do as I say."

Jakub gives me a big smile and trots alongside Connor. As we go, he tells me lots of random facts about wolves.

Asha is waiting for us on a swing in the play park. She has her back to the Skull brothers in the skate park. I can see them as they practise their tricks – flip-turns, drop-ins and flat-ground ollies. Asha looks Jakub up and down. "I thought this was going to be a secret," she says.

"I couldn't stop him," I say. "Connor told him."

"Jakub can talk wolf," says Connor.

At this, Jakub throws his head back and puts his hands to his mouth and howls.

"C'mon," I say.

We walk past the Skull brothers. Connor and Jakub race ahead of us, howling and yipping like wolf cubs. As we walk out of the park, I have the feeling Luke and Scott are watching us. Asha senses it too. She does a spin, then flips the board up to her hand. I don't dare try. I'd probably land flat on my back. It's only when we turn the corner at the end of the street that I turn and see Scott is standing at the top of the skateboard ramp watching us leave.

Chapter 3

The wolf is still at the old gasworks.

Somehow I thought he might have gone away or that maybe we had made him up in our heads. But he's still there, lying on the pile of sacks. He must have got up at some point, because the bread crusts Connor threw for him have gone. I look over at Jakub. His eyes are wide, wide open.

"It's a wolf," Jakub whispers as if he can't believe it. "A real wolf."

The wolf watches us too. He lifts up his nose and sniffs the air. Then he turns away and licks his lips.

"I told you," says Connor. "He wants to eat us."

Jakub shakes his head. "No," he says. "He's scared. If he looks away and licks his lips, it means he sees you as the top wolf."

"Are you sure?" I ask.

Jakub nods. "It's wolf language."

Jakub opens his book for me to see, and I look at pictures of wolves, some with tails and heads tucked low and others standing with their tails right up. Some of the wolves are snarling at each other and showing their teeth. "Ugh, I wouldn't want to get into a fight with a wolf," I say.

Jakub closes the book. "Wolves don't want to fight with each other. It's not worth the risk. That's why they use body language to sort out who's top wolf. They don't eat people either. That's just in fairy tales."

"If you know so much about wolves," says Asha, "then what's this one doing here?"

Jakub looks back at the wolf and shrugs. "I don't know. It shouldn't be here. The last wolf in Britain was killed in 1680."

"Well, this one's hungry," I say. I take a can of dog food from my bag and pull the ring to open it. I don't have a bowl, so I rip a spare page from my pad of paper and tip the meaty chunks out. I wrap it up and throw the whole thing to the wolf.

He scrabbles to his feet and limps towards the food.

"He's hurt his foot," says Asha.

The wolf doesn't put his front right paw on the ground. He sniffs at the food, then rips the paper with his teeth. He eats the meat in big greedy gulps. When he's finished, he turns and limps out of the warehouse. We follow him at a distance and watch him make his way slowly down to the river, where he laps at the water. His ears twitch forward and back, listening. Then we watch as he goes back into the warehouse and settles into the pile of sacks. He spins around and around before he flumps down with his head on his paws and turns to watch us again.

"We can't do any more for him at the moment," I say. "Best give him some space."

Asha nods. "C'mon, let's try out that ramp."

I grab my board and turn to Connor and Jakub. "Don't go near the wolf or you can't come back."

"Can we explore?" says Connor.

I nod. "Don't go near the river, OK?"

I watch them walk out into the wasteland. Then I turn back around to see Asha already at the top of the ramp ready to fly down. She pushes off and picks up speed, twisting between bricks and rubble.

"That was *so* cool," she says, a massive grin on her face. "C'mon. I'll race you."

We build obstacles and make mini ramps from old boards balanced on bricks, and we don't even notice the time pass until Connor and Jakub come running in. At first I think something's wrong. Connor is doubled over. He's shaking and there are tears running down

his face. It's only when I get close I see he's laughing.

Jakub is holding something in his cupped hands. "We found a farting beetle!" he shouts.

Connor explodes into laughter again.

Asha rolls her eyes. "What've you got?"

Connor tries to speak between gulping air. "When Jakub tried to pick it up, it actually farted and I'm not even joking. It stinks!"

Jakub opens his hands and we see a small beetle with bright-green metallic wings and a red body. It moves so quickly that Jakub has to let it scuttle from hand to hand.

"Don't let it go," says Connor. He puts his hand into his school bag and pulls out the notebook where he keeps all his drawings and notes about dinosaurs. He starts to draw the

beetle. "We have to find out what it is," he says.

I watch Connor draw the beetle next to his picture of a dinosaur feeding in a swamp.

Asha pulls out her phone. "It's got to have a name." She speaks out loud as she taps into Google on her phone. "Green farting beetle in London."

"You'll never find it," I say.

Her eyebrows shoot up in surprise. "It is here. It's actually here. It's called a Streaked bombardier beetle. It says it squirts acid and makes a farting sound. It's meant to be really, really rare."

"We found loads of others," says Connor. "D'you want to see?"

We leave our skateboards and follow Jakub and Connor outside to a pile of rubble. Jakub pulls up a stone, and about ten little green beetles scuttle away to find shelter under other rocks. Then he and Connor turn over other stones to look for more bugs.

Asha sits down in the shade of a bush. "It's so hot," she says. She slips off her shoes and socks, digs her toes into the dirt and stares at them. "When did we last do this?"

I look across at her. "Do what?" I ask.

"Go barefoot," she says.

"I don't know," I say. "Years ago maybe. It was probably in your garden."

Asha grins. "Do it. Do it now."

I kick off my shoes and pull off my socks. I press my feet against the ground and feel the warmth through my skin.

It feels good to touch the earth.

Asha sighs. "Just think, there was a day when we ran barefoot for the last time together and we didn't even know."

"Well, it's not today," I say. I stand up and grin. "Race you!"

Asha laughs and runs after me. The stones spike against my feet, but I don't stop until Asha catches hold of me and pulls me down. We lie in the long grass and catch our breath.

It feels like we're five years old again.

Asha picks the white puffball of a dandelion and holds it in front of me. "Blow and make a wish," she says.

I smile. Last time we did this, I think I wished I could ride on a unicorn. Wishes were easy back then. Now what do I wish for? To be more popular? To be clever? For Dad to find a job? To be a happy family like we were before? I don't know. I blow and watch the dandelion seeds drift up and away.

Asha closes her eyes. "I could sleep here all day."

I lie next to her and stare up at the sky. It's a pale hazy blue, criss-crossed by aeroplane vapour trails. It's quiet too. The drone of traffic and hum of city life seem so far, far away.

I feel my body sink against the small stones and soft grass. I dig my fingers deep into the earth, and it's as if everything is draining out of me. I lie still and listen to the lap of small waves from a riverboat and the pop of seed heads bursting in the heat.

Everything is quiet.

Everything is still.

For the first time in a long while I feel I can breathe.

I watch a heron flap above us, its wing beats slow and lazy. It's a huge bird, filling up the sky. It flies down to the river, its wings outstretched and its legs ready to land. It vanishes somewhere into the reeds in the old dock. As we lie still, the wasteland comes to life around us. A flock of small birds flurry down to a wide puddle. Butterflies dance in shafts of sunlight, and small bees buzz from flower to flower. Three cormorants fly low, heading up the river. I prop myself up on my elbows and just watch. The more I look, the more I see.

It's not a wasteland.

It's a lost world.

A hidden wilderness.

Connor must be thinking the same, because he folds his arms around his knees and says, "It's like the *Land That Time Forgot*."

I smile because it's one of Connor's favourite old movies, where explorers find a hidden world full of dinosaurs.

"We'll have to give it a name," says Asha. "It belongs to us now."

"It belongs to the wolf," says Jakub. "We'll call it Wolf Land."

*

"C'mon," says Asha. She sits up and brushes dirt from her legs. "We'll come back to Wolf Land tomorrow."

We walk back to collect our skateboards. I don't want anyone else to come here, ever. It's our secret. It's our escape from school and home, where no one can tell us what to do.

But I should have known it was too good to hope for. A moment later, we hear the rumble and clack of skateboards.

There are two people on the skateboard ramp.

Luke and Scott.

The Skull brothers.

Here, in our place.

In Wolf Land.

Chapter 4

I hang back, but Asha marches up to them.
"You can't come here. We were here first."

Luke flicks his skateboard with his foot and
catches it in one hand. He leans towards her.
"And who's going to stop us?"

Asha doesn't move. I'm not sure what she's
going to say, but then she turns and points at
me. "She is."

My eyes open wide. What does she want me
to do? Luke thinks she's being funny.

Asha folds her arms. "If you don't go, Izzy will set her wolf on you."

Luke laughs out loud. "Yeah, right."

I look at Scott, but he doesn't laugh. Instead, he's looking beyond me to the far side of the building, and I know our secret is out. I turn and see the wolf standing up. He's watching us all.

"See?" I say. I try to sound brave, but I can hear my voice shake. I think of wolf language in Jakub's book. Maybe it works for humans too. I try to stand tall. I put my hands on my hips to look even bigger and look right at Luke. I try to show him I'm not scared.

Luke frowns and turns to look back at the wolf again. It starts to walk towards us, limping on its front paw.

Luke takes a step back, but Scott can't take his eyes off it.

"He'll bite you if you don't leave us," says Connor.

Scott looks at me. "He's hurt."

It's the first time I've heard Scott say anything for a long time. I forgot how soft his voice is. He sounds like the old Scott from primary school, when we found a baby blackbird and tried to collect ants and worms to feed it. I suddenly feel bad. The wolf is in pain, and I haven't done anything to help him. "I'm looking after him," I say.

Scott frowns. "We can't leave him like this." He drops low and moves slowly, holding out his hand. The wolf lowers its head and sniffs the air.

"Scott!" Luke shouts at him. "Get away from it."

But it's as if Scott is wrapped up in the world of this wolf and can't hear anyone else at all. I feel a pang of jealousy. He's my wolf. I saw him first, not Scott. I don't want Scott to be the first one to touch him. Scott has his back to us, but I see him pull his skull and crossbones bandana from his head and slip it over the wolf's nose to muzzle him. Scott looks back at me. "Can you help me hold him, Izzy? I need to look at his paw."

I creep forward. I know I shouldn't do this. It's dangerous. It's stupid.

Asha thinks so too. "Look, we should just call a vet," she says.

"He can't bite with this on," says Scott.

I hold on to the wolf's neck, pushing my fingers into his fur. It feels rough on the outside, but the undercoat is soft and thick. I can feel his bones. I didn't realise he was so thin. Scott runs his hand down the wolf's leg to his paw, and he bends down to look at it closely.

"Hold him," says Scott. "He's got something in there."

The wolf gives a sharp yelp, then Scott holds up a long spike of glass. "He'll feel better now," he says. He makes a sign for me to back away, then slips the bandana from the wolf's nose and steps back too.

The wolf licks his paw, and when he turns to walk away he isn't lame any more.

"He wants feeding," says Scott. "He's thin."

"I *am* feeding him," I say.

I want to thank Scott, but I still feel jealous. He's my wolf. I found him. I look at Scott and see his face is red and blotchy.

Jakub peers at him. "Are you crying?"

"No," Scott mumbles.

"You are," says Jakub.

I give Jakub a shove. Sometimes he should learn to keep his thoughts inside his head.

But I can see Scott is crying. I remember how upset he was when we found the baby blackbird without its mum. We tried to save it, but we couldn't. Scott locked himself in the classroom cupboard and cried for hours after it died.

Luke steps in front of Jakub. "Just shut it, OK! He's not crying." Luke puts his skateboard on the ramp again and rolls it under his foot.

"You can't stay," Asha says. "Wolf Land is our place."

I nod. "You've got your own skate park."

Luke looks at us and then at the long ramp. This is much better than the skate park. We all know that. "What if we teach you some tricks?" Luke asks.

The silence is thick in the air between us.

It's as if Luke is looking for middle ground, like we're two different wolf packs trying to sort out territory without a fight.

I reckon Asha realises this too. She looks at me quickly. "What d'you think, Izzy?"

I shrug. "If they can teach us to do a flat-ground ollie, they can stay."

Luke looks at me. "Is that a deal?"

"Deal," I say.

Luke nods. "Go on then. Let's see what you're doing."

I walk over to the ramp and put my skateboard down. I feel embarrassed. I'll probably fall flat on my back, and Luke and Scott will laugh at me. I push off and try to jump with the board, but it doesn't stay with me.

Luke doesn't laugh. He watches me closely. "You're doing it wrong," he says. "As soon as you've flicked the tail end down, you need to drag the side of your front foot up the board. That gives you lift." He puts his board down and shows me. "Now you try."

I have another go, and the board actually lifts a little way from the ground.

Luke folds his arms and nods. "You've almost got it. Now do it again. And again. Just keep doing it."

I push off again, slamming the tail down and sliding my foot up the board. It lifts for a moment, and I am up in the air. The ground is a blur beneath me.

"Woohoooo!" I shout.

"That's it," Luke grins.

Scott gives me a thumbs-up.

"Go, Izzy!" Asha yells.

I'm only in the air for a second, but it actually feels as if I'm flying.

Chapter 5

Luke and Scott have been true to their word and taught us new tricks. We meet every day after school, and Luke sets up a new slalom course or a new ramp to practise jumps and turns. I can't wait for the summer holidays when we can come and spend all day here.

Asha is always quicker to pick up the tricks than me. She's the one to race Luke down the track and beat him on the slalom.

"And you said girls can't skate," she says after she wins another race against him.

Scott smirks at Luke. "Nan would kill you if she knew you'd said that."

Luke grins. "Don't tell her."

I haven't seen their nan for ages. I remember her at school plays, sitting at the back. She was a small fiery woman with dyed-black hair and bright-blue eyes. She used to teach swimming at the local pool too.

"She was a national swimmer," says Scott.

"Missed the Olympic team because of injury," says Luke.

I can hear the pride in their voices for their small fierce nan.

Asha sits on the ground and crosses her legs. "I haven't seen her at the pool. Does she still swim?"

Scott frowns. He picks at some weeds and curls the stems around his fingers. "She's not been well."

"What d'you mean?" Asha asks.

"C'mon," says Luke as he walks to the top of the ramp again. "Let's have another race."

I watch Luke. I'd never really noticed it before, but now I see how Luke always protects Scott – he changes the conversation or takes the taunts and insults. Luke fights the world, and Scott just shrinks away from it.

I sit with Scott and watch Asha and Luke race each other down the ramp.

"I'm sorry your nan's ill," I say.

Scott picks up a stone and scratches the point of it into the ground. "If she gets really sick, we won't be allowed to live with her."

"Can't you live with your mum?" I ask.

Scott scratches the stone deeper and makes long score marks in the ground. "She wants us to." He flings the stone across the building. "But Nan says our mum can't look after herself at the moment, so she won't be able to look after us too."

"What'll you do?" I say.

Scott shrugs and turns his head away from me. It seems that the wolf is listening too. He pads softly closer and lies down in the dirt near to us. Scott reaches out, and the wolf crawls closer and pushes his nose into Scott's hand.

I should tell Scott to stop, but Scott and the wolf seem to trust each other. Maybe they see something of themselves in each other.

"People don't like wolves," Scott says. His fingers trace along the soft fur of the wolf's nose. "They think they're trouble."

The wolf moves closer and rolls onto his back so that Scott can scratch his belly. He seems more like a dog today.

"I reckon he's run away," says Scott. "I reckon he's run away from somewhere bad and found that it's just as bad here. He's got no one."

"He's got us," I say.

Scott looks at me and smiles. For a moment it lights up his face. "Yeah," he says. "He's got us."

"We'll come every day," I say.

"Every day," says Scott.

We join the others, but I turn to look back at the wolf. He's watching us with his golden eyes. I hate leaving him. As we turn the corner, we hear a sound – a wild cry that belongs to some place far from here. It starts off softly and gets louder. It echoes in the air. It's a wolf howl, and it goes right through me.

I feel it deep inside.

We all stop to listen.

I can tell the others feel it too.

It's a wild call, tying us together somehow, wrapping around us.

Jakub answers first.

Then we all do.

We raise our own voices and howl back.

We are now part of each other.

Part of the same pack.

*

Each day, I look forward to going to Wolf Land.
We listen out for the wolf's call when he hears
us. Then our own howls mix with his in this
metal and concrete landscape. It feels as if we
change in the moment we slip under the wire
fence. It's as if we leave our normal selves
behind and become wolves. Wolf Land is our
territory, and no one can touch us here.

It's our freedom.

I haven't seen Connor as happy as he is
here for a long time. Connor and Jakub have
made a huge map of Wolf Land. Connor doesn't
draw dinosaurs now; instead, he draws all
the living things he finds here. He fills his
notebook with animals and plants. His beetle

pictures are the best. He's found ten different types. He draws in all the little details, like the fine hairs on a beetle's leg. Scott showed him how to shade his pictures so that they look 3D. Connor looked so proud when Scott told him he could be a proper artist one day. Jakub has a notebook too, and he fills that with cartoons of an action hero he calls Wolf Man. The hours fly by as Connor and Jakub poke under stones and scramble through the bushes.

This is our place now.

Scott opens up his bag and pulls out spray paint and a stencil.

"What's that for?" Asha asks.

"It's our sign," he says.

I watch him spray the black paint over the stencil, and when he pulls it away a wolf head is left printed on the ground.

"We could get in trouble for that," says Asha.

Luke shrugs. "It's not like it matters. Nobody cares about this place. Nobody else comes here."

But he's spoken too soon.

Maybe this place was too perfect to last.

Connor and Jakub come running into the building.

"Hide!" says Connor. "There are people out there."

We duck down and keep our heads low. I lift my head to look. Outside in the sunlight I see three men with hard hats.

"Did they see you?" I whisper.

"Don't know," says Connor.

Connor looks like he's about to cry. "I left my bag out there."

We watch as one of the men bends down and picks up Connor's bag. He looks around as if trying to see who left the bag there, then he pulls out Connor's notebook. He turns the pages slowly, looking at all the drawings.

The other two men have moved on. One is pointing to the river and then to the steel frames of the gas tanks, but the man with the notebook stays behind. He takes photos of the pages with his phone.

"Who d'you think they are?" says Asha.

I sink down and put my head in my hands. "I bet they're the ones that want to buy the place and turn it into shops and offices."

"They're going," whispers Connor. I hear the jangle of chains, then the rev of an engine as a car pulls away.

Connor runs to grab his book. He turns it over and over as if he can't believe he's got it back. "It's all here," he says.

I look at the book. I see that Connor's written "Wolf Land" on the front and put his name and address there too. I feel sick inside. The man now knows who we are.

Luke picks up his skateboard. "I bet they'll come back. Might as well make the most of it here while we can."

We practise our moves, but it feels different now, not as good.

The wolf is restless too, as if the new smells of other humans have made him feel twitchy.

He curls up in his bed, his nose in his fur, but his eyes watch our every move.

By the time we leave, black clouds hang low over the city.

Thunder rumbles in the distance. A storm is on the way.

Maybe the wolf feels it too, because this time when we leave, his cry sounds wild and high, as if in pain.

We slip home beneath a dark and stormy sky.

And it feels as if everything is about to change.

Chapter 6

The next day at school goes so slowly. Scott doesn't say a word. In class, he just sits and draws wolves. His wolves are always behind bars, thick black bars that he scratches into the paper.

I pick up Connor and Jakub on the way to the gasworks and catch up with the others as they squeeze through the gap in the fence. We're more careful this time, and we listen out for other people.

We keep in the shadows as we slip alongside the red-brick building and avoid the puddles left after a night's rain.

Scott comes to a stop and frowns. "We haven't heard him howl yet."

"Maybe he hasn't heard us," I say.

Scott cups his hands and cries a soft howl that carries across the ground, but there's no answer from the wolf. Scott howls again, and we stand in silence and strain our ears to pick up a sound.

"Maybe he's asleep," Asha says.

We make our way forward but stop again. A police car and a large white van are parked on the far side of the fence.

"Let's come back later," says Asha. "We don't want to be seen. We could get into trouble."

"We have to make sure they don't find our wolf," I say.

Scott and I creep forward ahead of the others. As we turn and peer into the building, we see four people crowded around something on the ground. There are two policemen and two other men. One has a long pole with a hoop at the end, and the other is the man who took photos of Connor's notebook. One of the policemen takes a step back, and we all see a large wire cage.

Inside the cage is our wolf. He fills up all the space, and he's fighting to find a way out.

Before I can stop him, Scott runs towards the men, his feet flying across the ground. I don't know what to do, so I follow him and hear the others behind me.

"Let him go," yells Scott. He's trying to reach the cage, but one of the policemen holds him back.

"Steady, lad," the policeman says. "There's a dangerous animal here."

"He's ours," yells Scott. "You can't take him."

Scott is trying to break free. But the policeman is holding him firmly.

Connor steps forward and juts his chin out. "He's our wolf – we found him."

Jakub nods. "Let him go," he shouts.

I glance at Asha. It's over – we both know that. We can't stop them. They're going to take our wolf. They can't let him stay here.

Luke knows this too. He takes hold of Scott. "Leave it, Scott. We can't stop them."

"No," yells Scott. He's fighting Luke now. "They can't take him. They'll lock him up. He'll die."

The wolf is twisting in the cage. He bites at the bars to try to escape.

Scott turns to me. "Don't let them take him, Izzy," he shouts. "Don't let them."

There is nothing I can do. I stand back and watch the men lift and carry our wolf in the cage to the van. Connor presses his head against me. I feel his tears soak through my shirt.

The men walk away with the cage and our wolf inside it. We hear him howl. I want to howl back. I want to scream and shout. But the van doors slam shut, the engine revs up and the van pulls away into the traffic.

One of the policemen folds his arms and looks at us. "Didn't you read the signs? It's very dangerous to enter unsafe buildings. You're trespassing too."

69

The other policeman takes out his notebook and pencil. "We'll need names and addresses. We'll have to speak to your parents and carers and your school about this."

Jakub breaks into a sob, and Asha puts her arm around him.

I hold back the tears until the policeman leads us out of the gasworks, then I let myself cry.

We walk in silence and go our separate ways. We can't come back here again, ever. Even if we could, it wouldn't be the same. It's lost its magic.

In no time the developers will move in and rip it down and build their shops and offices.

There'll be no space for the cormorant or the heron, or Connor's farting beetles.

And there'll be no space for us.

What we had has been lost.

Wolf has gone, and with him the wild.

Chapter 7

Connor and I sit in my bedroom with our backs against my door and listen to the voices talking in the kitchen. The police officers have been here for about half an hour, telling Mum and Dad about how they found us in the gasworks. We hear the front door slam, and I get up, cross to the window and see them leave.

"Izzy! Connor! Get down here!" Dad shouts up the stairs.

"I want to be back in Wolf Land," Connor whispers.

"Me too," I say.

"Izzy! Connor!"

I stand up and help Connor get up too. "Come on. Let's get it over with."

Mum sits us down at the kitchen table, and Dad leans against the worktop.

"What were you thinking?" Dad snaps. "You're old enough to know better."

"'You lied to me, Isabelle," Mum says.

"I didn't," I say. "I never said I hadn't been to the gasworks."

Mum takes a sip of coffee, but she keeps looking right at me. "Don't play games with me. You know what I mean."

Dad leans forward. "You didn't just put yourself in danger but Connor too."

I stare down at my hands. "We were fine."

"I've had Jakub's father on the phone," says Mum. "What if something had happened to him?"

"He wanted to come," says Connor.

"That's not the point," Mum snaps. "I trusted Izzy to look after you." She leans forward and raps her finger on the table. "And I heard Luke and Scott were there too. Haven't I told you to keep away from them? They're both trouble."

I look up at Mum and scowl. "You're like everyone else. You're wrong about them."

Mum sits back and folds her arms. "Really? I heard Scott sprayed graffiti all over the gasworks."

"He paints wolves," says Connor. "He helped me draw my animals."

I nod. "Show them, Connor," I say. "Show Mum and Dad your notebook. Show them what you've done."

Connor runs to his room and brings back the notebook. He pushes it across the table.

Dad brushes it to one side. "You don't get it, do you? You could have been killed in there."

"And what would you care?" I shout. "You wouldn't even notice."

I expect Dad to get mad at me, but he just stands there. I can't tell what he's thinking.

"That's enough, Izzy," says Mum softly.

"It's true," I say. "Dad never wants to do anything with us any more. He doesn't even

want us here. It's why we went to the gasworks anyway." It's a horrible thing to say, but right now I don't care.

Mum puts a hand on my arm. "Izzy, I said that's enough."

Connor has picked up his notebook and is tearing pages out, crumpling them up in his fists.

"Don't, Connor," I say. I try to stop him, but he shoves the whole book in the bin. "No point," he sobs. "Wolf Land is gone. Our wolf is gone too."

Mum stares after Connor. "And what about this wolf? Is it true there was a wolf?"

"I'm going to bed," I say. My head is hurting and all my thoughts are spinning so fast that I can't think straight. I can't speak to Mum or Dad. How can I tell them about the wolf? How

can I tell them what he meant to all of us when they just don't listen?

Mum watches me leave. "Come back, Isabelle. I haven't finished."

I ignore her and keep walking up the stairs.

"The head teacher wants to see you in her office first thing tomorrow," she says. "The police will be there. They're going to talk to the whole school at assembly too."

"Fine," I say.

Mum follows me to the door. "Izzy, doesn't this worry you?"

I shrug and close the door, shutting her out. The truth is I feel empty. I feel lost without our wolf.

I don't really feel anything at all.

Chapter 8

Mrs Stone's office is too small for the two police officers, as well as Asha, Luke, Scott and me.

Mrs Stone begins with a lecture about the dangers of unsafe buildings. She lists the grim ways we could have been injured or died and tells us the police officers will be giving a talk to the whole school about safety. She looks around at us all. "No one is allowed near the gasworks. Is that understood?"

I nod and stare at my feet.

"Any questions?" she says.

I don't dare ask a question, but I see Asha put her hand up. "So, where *can* we go?" she says.

Mrs Stone frowns. "What do you mean?"

"Well," says Asha. "There's nothing round here. There's nothing to do."

"There's the sports centre," says Mrs Stone.

"Can't afford it," says Asha.

"There are lots of after-school clubs that are free," says Mrs Stone. "You could join some of those. There are lots of things to do."

"It's still school," says Luke.

Mrs Stone shakes her head. "The clubs are fun. You and Scott should come to some."

"It's not the same," I say.

Mrs Stone rolls her eyes. "Why not?" She looks annoyed with me now. "You can still see your friends."

I look at Asha, Luke and Scott, hoping they can help me out, but they don't say anything.

I think of Asha and me lying in the long grasses blowing dandelion seeds and making wishes. I turn back to Mrs Stone. "When you were our age, where did you go?"

Mrs Stone frowns at me. "Izzy, what are you on about?"

"Did you ever have somewhere away from school and home? Somewhere you ran barefoot with your friends?" I ask.

Mrs Stone sits back in her chair. "Well, I was lucky. We had woods at the back of our road. My friends and I spent hours together there."

"What happened to *them?*" I ask.

"Well, we all grew up and moved on," says Mrs Stone.

"I mean the woods," I say. "What happened to them?"

Mrs Stone frowns. "There are houses built there now."

"But you remember what it felt like, running wild in those woods?" I say.

"Of course," she says.

"If you could go back in time and see yourself there, what would you say? How could you tell you and your friends that the woods have gone? How would you tell them that there would be a day they would play in there for the last time?"

81

Mrs Stone opens her mouth and then closes it again. A breeze flaps the window blinds, and it's as if a small piece of wild has slipped into the room with us.

"We're losing our wild place too," I say.

"This isn't the point, Izzy," says Mrs Stone. "You put yourselves at risk in the gasworks. You went near a wild animal too. It's a good thing it was caught before it bit one of you."

"Where is he now?" asks Scott. "Where's our wolf?"

Mrs Stone looks at him. "I don't know, Scott."

Scott shakes his head. "You must know."

"My concern is for your safety, not the wolf," she says.

Scott bangs his fist on the desk. "Where's our wolf?"

Mrs Stone stands up. "Scott, I think you had better leave the room to cool down a bit."

Scott walks out and slams the door behind him.

Mrs Stone sighs. "I think we've finished this meeting."

"We have to know what happened to our wolf," I say.

One of the policemen steps forward. "I'll find out," he says. "I'll find out and let you know."

*

We sit through assembly and morning lessons. I stand in the line for lunch, but Asha finds

me and says Mrs Stone wants to see us in her office again. Luke and Scott are there too. There's someone else in the office too. It's the man we saw at the gasworks who took photos of Connor's notebook. He was there when our wolf was captured.

"This is Finn Evans," says Mrs Stone. "The policemen put him in contact with us today because he can tell you about the wolf. He wants to tell you about the plans for the gasworks too."

I turn to the man and scowl. "You want to turn the gasworks into shops and offices."

"Listen to him, Izzy," Mrs Stone says. "I think you'll want to hear what he has to say."

Finn Evans smiles at us. "I work for a wildlife charity. We've been trying to buy the gasworks and the land that goes with it and

turn it into a nature reserve. We have other brownfield sites along the Thames."

"Brownfield?" I say.

"Brownfield sites are ones that have already been built on," says Finn. "Some sites are good for wildlife, especially for insects. The picture your brother drew of a bombardier beetle confirmed that the gasworks site is one we'd love to have. City nature reserves become space for wildlife." He pulls a piece of paper from his folder and opens it out to show a map of the gasworks and the land around it. "This is what we'd like to do with the gasworks site," he says.

We crowd around the map. It shows paths and walkways around ponds and alongside the river. The red-brick building has been replaced with a smaller building with a label that says *Visitor centre and coffee shop.*

"So you mean it's going to stay wild?" I say.

"That's the plan," says Finn. "But we haven't been able to buy the land yet. We might need your help. That's why I wanted to see you."

"Don't ask us," I say. "We haven't got any money."

Finn laughs. "It's not your money we want. Two elderly sisters own the land. We need to convince them to sell it to us. It's our last chance. A big property tycoon is offering them loads of money for it. If we could show the Norton sisters the drawings Connor did, it might help them see what we could do with the land. It would be great if we could use some of the drawings – or anything else you can think of. We have a meeting with them next week."

"What about our wolf?" says Scott. "Where's he now?"

"He's safe," says Finn.

"He can't live in a cage. It'll kill him," says Scott.

Finn smiles. "He won't have to. He's going to live in Scotland, where he'll be able to run across mountains."

"He's a wolf," says Asha. "You can't just set him free."

Finn shakes his head. "He's not a wolf. Well, not completely."

Scott looks at me, then at Finn. "What d'you mean?"

"He's a wolf-dog," says Finn. "He's a cross between a wolf and a dog. A lot of people want a wolf-dog because they think they look cool or tough, but actually they can be difficult to look after. They have the wild in them. People love

87

the puppies but can't cope with them when they become young dogs."

"So where is he now?" says Scott.

"Wolf-Dog Rescue have him until he's put on some weight, but I have a friend in Scotland who wants to give him a permanent home. He's had wolf-dogs before."

Scott pushes his hands deep in his pockets. "So he'll be OK?"

"He'll be more than OK," says Finn. He smiles. "I'll get my friend to send photos."

Luke shakes his head. "So you mean he isn't really a wolf at all?"

"He's part wolf," says Finn. "Part wild."

Like us, I want to say. The wild is in us too.

Maybe even a city can be part wild.

The land around the gasworks is still a wild space, even without our wolf.

We've been given the chance to save it.

I turn to Finn. "We'll help," I say. "We want to see the Norton sisters too."

Chapter 9

I run to get Connor from school and hurry him home. I want to rescue his notebook from the bin. Maybe we can save some of the pages. We'll need them to show the Norton sisters if we want to ask them to help turn the gasworks into a nature reserve.

But it's too late.

I forgot it was bin day. The bin is empty. The rubbish has already been put out and collected. Connor's notebook with all his drawings will have been pulped and crushed and piled onto the tip.

"I could do some more," says Connor.

I nod, but I know he won't have time. It won't be the same anyway. Even his drawings had the wild in them. "I'll make us some toast," I say.

I try to sound cheerful for Connor's sake, but I feel bored and hollow. Our one chance of trying to make the Norton sisters change their minds has gone. Now there's nowhere to go. Nothing to do. Connor dumps his bag on the floor and flicks on the TV. Mum's working till six, and there's no sign of Dad – and I'm glad he's not here.

We sit watching cartoons and eating more toast. Mum will come home and cook tea. We'll go to bed, wake up and do the same all over again the next day and the day after that. For ever. I feel empty, like there's a wolf-shaped hole inside me.

I hear a key in the door and look at the clock. It's not six yet. But it's not Mum back home, it's Dad. Connor flicks off the TV and slides from his chair, ready to go to his room. We don't want to stick around for Dad to tell us off again.

Dad fills the kitchen doorway before we have time to leave. He's carrying two shopping bags that block our exit too.

"I bought pizza for tonight," he says, lifting one up. "I thought Mum could do with a break."

I look over at Connor to check it's not just me hearing things. Dad never cooks.

"I got these as well," he says, walking over. He heaves the bag up, and it thumps heavily on the table. "I've got books."

We watch him pull the books out of the bag and stack them high. Books about trees and insects and birds.

He smiles and stares at them as if they're pirate booty. "Do you know," he says, "I've borrowed them from the library? The amazing thing is that it was all free. Free books. Just think of that."

I frown. "I know, Dad. It's a library."

Dad shakes his head and smiles. "Brilliant, isn't it, when you think about it. And I've never had a library card before. I've never even been in the library before."

Connor has picked up a book on insects and is turning over the pages, looking at bright beetles of all colours and shapes.

"I thought we could look at them together," says Dad. "I've got this too." He pulls a notebook from his pocket.

I just stare at it.

It's Connor's notebook.

I take it from him and flick through it. The crumpled pages have been flattened and carefully stuck back in. There's a tomato stain on the corner of the cover, but otherwise it's perfect. I want to hug Dad, but it feels so long since the last time that I hug Connor's notebook instead. "We need this," I say. "We need this to save Wolf Land."

"Wolf Land?" says Dad.

I nod, but before I can tell him about it Connor is talking and telling him about all the things he and Jakub have found. Connor takes the notebook and shows Dad his drawings of

beetles. And Dad is listening. I mean really listening. He's wrapped up in Connor's world.

I smile and a warm feeling spreads right through me.

We may have lost our wolf, but I can't help but think our wolf has helped us to find our dad.

Chapter 10

It turns out the Norton sisters want to meet us
too. Finn has fixed for us to meet them at the
gasworks. I feel sick with nerves, and we look
an odd group as we stand outside the locked
gates. Dad insisted he wanted to come with us,
and Jakub has come with his dad too. Asha is
here with her skateboard under her arm. Luke
and Scott said they'd come, but they're not here
yet.

I'm not sure what I expect the Norton
sisters to look like. They must be really rich
to own the land here. Maybe they'll arrive
in a posh limousine. Maybe they won't even

step out of it. But then a taxi pulls up, and two elderly ladies step out. Dad and Finn walk over and offer to help them across the uneven ground, but I see the taller sister wave them away.

"They look so old," whispers Jakub.

"Shh!" hisses Asha.

I feel so nervous. I can tell Connor does too. He clutches his notebook tight against his chest.

Finn introduces us to Margaret and Alice Norton. Margaret's the older sister. She looks the serious one. Alice smiles more but lets her sister do the talking.

Margaret Norton stares at us over her gold-rimmed glasses. "So you're the children who have been trespassing on our land."

I don't know what to say. I glance at Asha, then stare down at my feet.

Finn steps forwards. "Connor, why don't you lead the way and show the Norton sisters what you've found?"

Finn hands out hard hats to wear, then unlocks the gates and we follow Connor and Jakub. Finn tells the sisters about the plans for the nature reserve and points out where ponds and pathways would be. He asks Connor and Jakub to show us the stones where the Streaked bombardier beetles live. Dad proudly opens Connor's notebook and shows the sisters the drawings. Jakub is keen to show his Wolf Man cartoons too. I want to tell Jakub to put them away, but Alice Norton seems to like looking at them. She asks him lots of questions. She loves talking about the cormorants and herons too.

Margaret Norton turns to Asha and me. "What about you two?"

Asha turns her skateboard over in her hands. "We come here to skate."

Margaret frowns. "Can't you do that at home?" she says.

Asha shakes her head. "It's just roads. The skate park is too small for everyone."

"It's not just us," I say. I point to the gates where we can see Luke and Scott walking over to us. "We'd all love a skateboard park right here."

Margaret waits for Luke and Scott to reach us. "Let's see what you can do then," she says.

Luke doesn't wait for a moment. He drops his board and pushes off along the concrete,

does an ollie over a pile of rubble and a flick-spin.

Alice laughs. "I wish we'd had those in our day."

Margaret doesn't seem so impressed. She turns around and looks at the gasworks and the river beyond. "You do realise," she says to Finn, "that if we sell this land to you, we will lose a lot of money. We could sell this land for ten times the money you are offering."

There's a silence, then Jakub speaks. "But what would you do with all that money? You'll die before you can spend it all."

There's an even deeper silence, and Asha shoves Jakub in the back. But it's too late. Jakub can't keep his thoughts inside his head. What has been said can't be unsaid. Margaret's frown deepens.

But Alice laughs. "That's exactly what I said to you, Margaret. At least this boy is honest, not like that property tycoon."

Margaret scowls. "Yes, he was a nasty little man. He tried to sell us a posh house in Chelsea. I told him we're quite happy where we are, with our friends and neighbours."

"Please let us have the land instead," I say. "It's not just for us. It's for the animals too."

Margaret looks over her glasses at us. "What would you miss if you didn't have it?" she asks. It's a direct question that demands an answer.

"Exploring," says Jakub.

"I'd miss skateboarding," says Asha.

"Same," says Luke.

Scott is staring at his feet, and his face is bright red. He hates everyone looking at him. "Friends," he mumbles.

Connor reaches up and clings to Dad's sleeve. "I want to come beetle hunting with Dad."

Margaret seems to soften. "You're lucky. Our father spent his life trying to make money. He ended up a very rich man, but we hardly saw him. We had plenty of things, but we didn't have him."

"What about you, Izzy?" says Alice. "What would you miss?"

I take a deep breath in. There's so much to say. I try to think what I love the most here. It's been our wild place, somewhere we haven't been told what to do or been marked or graded by school. Even friendship hasn't been

measured in the number of likes. It's been real. I think of running barefoot with Asha across the grass. I now know what our wolf gave us and what we would miss.

"Well?" says Margaret.

"Freedom," I say. "Freedom to run wild."

There's a pause when no one speaks. A grasshopper chirps in the grasses and a flock of small birds whirrs past.

Alice smiles. "I can't speak for my sister," she says, "but I like the thought of leaving a piece of wilderness in the city, somewhere for people too."

We all look at Margaret. It's up to her now.

She looks across the old gasworks site as if she is imagining what it could be. "I'd like that," she says. She turns to Alice and smiles.

"And who knows. We might even live long enough to enjoy it too."

*

We watch the Norton sisters leave by taxi, and I breathe out slowly. I can't quite believe what has happened. No one can. Dad takes my hand and squeezes it as we walk out of the gasworks. I stop to look back at the crumbling concrete and rusted rail tracks. I try to picture in my head a different skyline when the metal frames of the gasworks have been torn down, when tall trees fringe the horizon instead. Cormorants and herons will make their nests here. Finn says that in the winter, flocks of migrating geese and ducks will come to rest and feed in the ponds, and in the summer, swallows and swifts will skim for water. He says we'll have kingfishers too.

Finn says it will be magical.

He says it will be for everyone.

I know he's right.

Everything will change.

Everything has changed.

Yet, I still feel like I've lost something. It was our place, our world for just a while.

And now our wolf has gone.

I feel tears prick my eyes and look up into the clear blue sky.

Maybe the wolf was part of the change. Maybe we needed him to give us new ways to see.

Bright puffy clouds slide across the sky, pushed by a fresh wind. Their cloud shadows slip beneath them, dark shapes that race each

other across the ground. For a moment the cloud shadows look like wolves, and I feel my heart skip a beat.

And I know that the wolf is always here inside.

Like an imprint of some other wilderness.

We only need to look to find it.

And to remember.

There is another side to us.

We are part wolf.

Part wild.

Our books are tested
for children and young people by
children and young people.

Thanks to everyone who consulted on
a manuscript for their time and effort in
helping us to make our books better
for our readers.